MONOTH
THE SPIKED DESTROYER

With special thanks to Allan Frewin Jones

www.seaquestbooks.co.uk

ORCHARD BOOKS
338 Euston Road, London NW1 3BH
Orchard Books Australia
Level 17/207 Kent St, Sydney, NSW 2000

A Paperback Original
First published in Great Britain in 2015

Series created by Beast Quest Limited, London

Text © Beast Quest Limited 2015
Cover and inside illustrations by Artful Doodlers,
with special thanks to Bob and Justin © Orchard Books 2015

A CIP catalogue record for this book is available from
the British Library.

ISBN 978 1 40833 477 5

1 3 5 7 9 10 8 6 4 2

Printed in Great Britain

The paper and board used in this paperback are natural recyclable
products made from wood grown in sustainable forests. The
manufacturing processes conform to the environmental regulations of
the country of origin.

Orchard Books is an imprint of Hachette Children's Group and
published by The Watts Publishing Group Limited, an Hachette UK
company.

www.hachette.co.uk

MONOTH
THE SPIKED DESTROYER

BY ADAM BLADE

ORCHARD

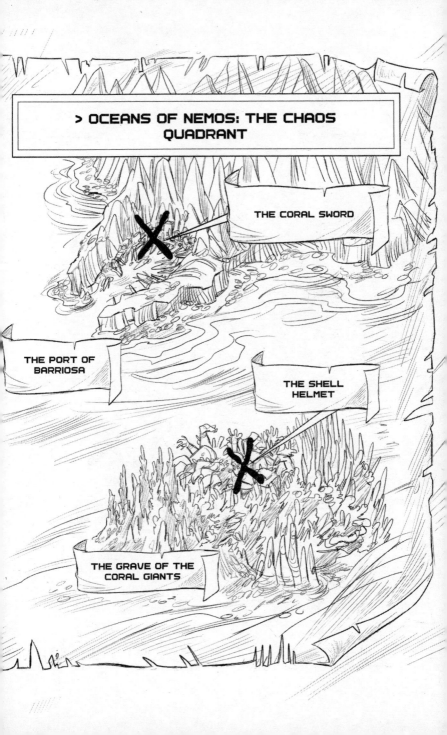

I have waited in the shadows long enough, perfecting myself. Now I will strike at my wretched enemies and make all Nemos bow before me. All I need to complete my plan are the Arms of Addulis: the Spear, the Breastplate, the Sword and the Helmet.

My mother used to tell me stories of their power, and for a long time I thought they were myths. But now I know they are real, buried in this vast ocean and waiting for a new master to wield them. With the Arms of Addulis in my control, no Merryn or human will be able to stop me.

But... I almost hope there is some pathetic hero foolish enough to try. My Robobeasts are ready — unlike anything these oceans have witnessed before. My enemies will learn that their flesh is weak.

Quake before your new leader!

RED EYE

CHAPTER ONE

THE GRAVE
OF THE
CORAL GIANTS

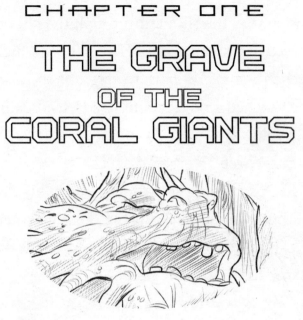

Max worked to repair the corroded and weakened hull of the *Lizard's Revenge*, his jaw set, his muscles aching and the sweat running down his face. He was strapped into a harness that hung from the ship's bow. He clutched a soldering gun, and was welding reinforcement panels over the holes created by Venor the Sea Scorpion's acidic venom.

At least the engines are still working well, he

thought as the ship cut through the choppy waves in pursuit of the *Hive*, Siborg's high-tech lab-ship. *We have to keep our speed up.* He touched a finger to his headset, adjusting the volume.

Beep. Beep.

Rivet's homing signal was clear in his ears. Max was anxious about the dogbot's safety. The loyal robot had used his paw magnets to clamp himself to the hull of the *Hive*.

Max was still smarting from the trick Siborg had played on them. A device had been secretly attached to the ankle of Max's pirate companion Roger's six-year-old niece, Grace. Siborg had told them it was a bomb, and that he would detonate it if they didn't hand over the precious Arms of Addulis that they had gathered.

Max had reluctantly surrendered the ancient artefacts: the Pearl Spear, the Stone

Breastplate and the Coral Sword, only for Siborg to reveal the bomb was a fake!

Now Siborg had three of the four Arms of Addulis, the battle-gear used long ago by the great Merryn warrior. All he needed was the Shell Helmet – forged from the ancient remains of a mystical sea creature. Once he had the full set, he'd be invincible.

"Max, how are the repairs going?" It was Lia's voice in his headset. She was on the bridge with Roger.

"I'm almost finished," Max replied, glancing down to see Spike, Lia's faithful swordfish, leaping from the water as he sped alongside the ship.

"Have you any idea who Siborg really is under that battle suit?" asked Lia.

"I don't," Max admitted. "And I don't understand how he knows so much about me." Siborg took pleasure in taunting Max, telling him he was as gullible as his mother, and making references to his uncle, the wicked Professor. Max angrily hammered a final plate into place. "He's been one step ahead of us from the very start of the Quest."

"He still needs the Helmet," said Lia. "I've seen old pictures of it in the Royal Palace in Sumara. It's very beautiful, and it gives the

wearer Aqua Powers far stronger than that of any Merryn." Her voice trembled. "Imagine what Siborg could do if he had the helmet and could control every creature in the sea."

"He'd be unstoppable," agreed Max, touching a control pad on his wrist unit. A powerful winch whisked him up to deck level.

He strode along the deck and climbed the steep steps to the bridge.

"Stand and deliver, you scurvy swab!" cried Grace, barring Max's way, her tricorn hat at a jaunty angle on her ribboned hair and a toy blaster in her hand.

"I surrender!" grinned Max, putting his hands up.

Grace was like a pirate in miniature with her yellow silk blouse and her trousers tucked into leather boots. She even wore an eye patch, although it covered a perfectly good eye – just as her Uncle Roger's did.

"I was only practising for when we get to those bilge-rat cyrates!" Grace explained, shoving her blaster into her wide belt. "Is there something I can do until we catch up with them?"

"She's been restless for a while," Roger said to Max, a slightly weary smile coming over his craggy face. "I'll tell you what, my little powder monkey," he said to her, his hands resting on the ship's wheel. "Why don't you go down to the hold and sift through all the booty. Pick out the most valuable things." He winked at Max and Lia. "If the *Lizard's Revenge* goes down, we'll need to get our hands on the good stuff as quickly as possible."

"Humph," said Grace, her fists on her hips. "Sounds like you want to get rid of me."

"Not at all," said Lia, resting her webbed

hand on Grace's shoulder. "It's very important work."

Grace gave her a thoughtful look then shrugged. "Okay," she said. "But if anything exciting happens up here, you have to let me know! Promise?"

"We promise," said Roger, giving Max a wink with his one visible eye.

Grace clattered down the stairs to the hold.

Max walked over to the ship's high-tech control panel and peered at the scanner. It showed two bright points in the great empty expanse of the ocean. One was the *Lizard's Revenge* – and the other was Siborg's lab-ship, the *Hive*. Max drew in a sharp breath as he saw that the leading blip on the scanner was no longer moving.

"Siborg's stopped," he said. "Roger, cut the engines. We don't want to be seen."

Roger tapped at a set of touchpads and the

growl of the ship's engines died away. The *Lizard's Revenge* settled on the sea, drifting slowly forwards.

"I'm going to take the hydrodisk to investigate," said Max.

Roger eyed him uncertainly. "Is that wise, shipmate?" he growled.

Lia stepped forward. "I'll go with you," she said to Max. She looked at Roger. "We have to do this."

Max steered the hydrodisk at high speed through the ocean while Lia rode Spike alongside.

"There's something strange down there," came Lia's voice in Max's headset. Spike gave a flick of his tail and sped downwards with the Merryn girl on his back.

Max frowned and he followed. He could see curious curling shapes in the depths –

strange, pale tangles of growth that reminded him of the bare branches of trees.

But then, as he dived closer, he saw what it was. "It's coral!" he said in surprise. "A whole forest of coral!"

"But this isn't normal coral," said Lia in an awed voice. "Look more closely."

Max steered the hydrodisk through the twisting and twining branches of coral. He widened his eyes as he began to see shapes among them, like arms and feet, limbs and skeletal heads, all jumbled up among the coral branches.

"What is this place?" Max gasped.

"I've heard of it," came Lia's worried voice. "It's called the Grave of the Coral Giants. The old tales say that Addulis was able to summon the Giants in times of need."

Normally Max would have thought such legends were just stories told to frighten

children, but some of the limbs did look awfully realistic.

As he steered his way cautiously through the eerie forest, he felt the water quake and saw coral shudder around him.

"Max?" Roger's urgent voice was in his headset. "There's something big down there with you. It's on the sensor, but I can't make out what it is. Be careful, shipmate."

Max touched the screen of his control

panel. Rivet's signal was coming to him loud and clear, but it seemed to be broadcasting from deep within the coral forest.

"How can the *Hive* have made its way through all this coral without leaving any trace?" Max asked Lia. Lia ducked low to Spike's back as the slender fish wound its way through the branches.

"I don't know," she said.

With Lia and Spike close by, Max followed

the signal, cautiously steering the hydrodisk through the narrowing tangle of bent coral bodies. Shapes like unmoving hands jutted from the sand, reaching towards them.

It feels like the coral is closing in on us, Max thought, peering uneasily through the glass shield.

"I see something!" cried Lia. Suddenly Spike darted downwards. Max followed close behind. They were moving along the ocean floor now, the water filled with thick limbs of coral.

Max saw a familiar shape lying in the silt. "Rivet!" he cried.

He switched off the hydrodisk's engine and climbed out, then swam down to where the dogbot lay on one side, bound with heavy ropes.

What has Siborg done to him?

Lia and Spike hovered above as Max

searched Rivet's controls.

"His power systems have been disabled," he said. "The tracker signal is the only thing left working."

Why did Siborg allow me to find Rivet? It makes no sense.

Max made some speedy adjustments. Rivet's eyes lit up and he struggled in his bonds.

"Max! Ambush!" the dogbot shouted.

Even as Max reached for his hyperblade, he saw a dozen sleek shapes powering towards him through the coral.

Cyrates!

They were coming in from all sides. And as they sped forwards, they reached out with their arms and deadly blasters slid out of their robotic hands.

CHAPTER TWO

CYRATE ATTACK

Max drew his hyperblade as the cyrates closed in. With streamlined limbs, their silver bodies streaked through the water. Their red eyes gleamed with menace as they aimed their blasters.

They've been upgraded, and we're outnumbered! This is going to be really tough!

Max readied himself for a ferocious battle as the cyrates circled them. Siborg's voice rang in his headset.

"I see you've fallen into yet another of my traps," he said. "Will you never learn?"

Max gritted his teeth.

"Did you really think your dogbot could attach himself to the hull of my lab-ship without me noticing?" Siborg said. "I only let him come this far to bring you within the grasp of my most brutal Robobeast yet."

"I'm not scared of you or your creations!" shouted Max, brandishing his hyperblade.

"You should be," came the voice. "The Helmet of Addulis is buried beneath this coral forest, and Monoth will soon find it. And then I will have all four of the ancient artefacts!"

The seabed shook again under Max's feet. But a plan was already forming in his mind. He pressed the hydrodisk's fetchpad and heard its engines roar into life. But would it arrive in time?

"Cyrates," said Siborg calmly. "Kill these meddling pests."

Max and Lia darted aside to avoid the searing jets from the blasters. Before the cyrates could fire again, the speeding hydrodisk smashed through them. It sliced one clean in half and sent another tumbling to the ground, its electronics hissing and spitting as it broke apart.

Max swung his hyperblade in a wide arc, its keen edge slicing through the ropes that bound Rivet's legs.

"Blast them, Rivet!" he shouted. The dogbot roared up from the seabed, aiming his rear thrusters at the cyrates and sending three of them spinning helplessly through the water.

"Spike, to me!" cried Lia, leaping up as the swordfish swept in between her legs. Spike carried her away as a blaster sent up a spray of silt where she had been standing.

Max flung himself at the remaining cyrates, ducking more blasts. He felt the hot sting of a ray as it grazed his forehead. He stabbed his hyperblade into a cyrate's chest, feeling it cut through wires and transistors.

As the cyrate dropped to the seabed, Max

saw Lia leap from Spike's back and fall upon another of their attackers. She clung to its shoulders as it writhed and struggled under her. She grabbed the head between both hands and gave a sharp twist. Short-circuited electronics flickered as the disabled cyrate went limp in the water.

Another blast burned close to Max's arm, but he grasped the cyrate's weapon and wrenched it upwards so the next burst of fire cut harmlessly through the water.

He could see more shapes speeding in through the tunnels of coral. How many cyrates did Siborg have?

He turned in the water, aiming the cyrate's blaster at the approaching droids. Spike came shooting through the coral, his long spear jabbing into the throat of one of the cyrates, almost slicing its head off.

We have to escape this trap!

"Lia! Rivet! This way!" Max shouted. He swam rapidly through a long tunnel of coral branches, Rivet at his side and Lia and Spike right behind them.

He glanced over his shoulder to see the remaining cyrates pursuing them, red eyes burning, blasters shooting out their deadly beams.

Max had an idea. Rivet was outfitted with a spool of fine microcord. Made from incredibly tough nanofibre, it was perfect for the fishing the dogbot was designed for.

"Rivet – give me your paw!"said Max. He unwound the microcord. "Now, Rivet, go to the right! Quickly. And hide!" Rivet sped away as Max swam left, stretching out the fine cord between them. Max ducked behind a chunk of coral, peering from cover, his heart racing.

The cyrates slowed, their heads turning

from side to side, obviously searching for him and Rivet.

"Now, Rivet!" cried Max, shooting from his hiding place. "Swim around them!" Rivet burst out from behind the coral, swimming at top speed.

They circled the surprised cyrates, pulling the cord tight around them so that the struggling creatures were crammed together. Blaster bursts exploded among them and pieces of metal spun through the water as the cyrates shot one another in the confusion.

Max grinned as the defeated cyrates sank to the ground.

"Siborg!" he shouted. "Is that all you've got?" Max felt the seabed shuddering under him.

No! What's happening now?

The ground shook more wildly, bulging upwards, sand and silt sliding away. A moment later, the seabed erupted, sending pieces of coral flying through the water.

Max stared in shock as a huge spinning drill drove upwards from beneath the seabed.

"What is that?" cried Lia, shrinking back from the whirling drill.

Max gave a gasp of shock and dismay as a gigantic form burst up from beneath the sand, its terrifying roars making the ocean shake.

He flung his hands over his ears to try and block out the noise. The creature was almost too huge for him to take in.

The grinding drill formed the tusk of an immense narwhal. Its head was covered by a fearsome, sharp-edged metal shield, its great body armoured with silver spikes. The mouth gaped, filled with ferocious dagger-like teeth, its throat like a black cavern.

Crazed red eyes glared from under the

robotic helmet, swivelling wildly until they locked on Max and Lia.

It roared again and Max was driven back by the pounding of the disturbed water.

"It's Siborg's latest Robobeast!" he shouted, his heart thundering in his chest, his blood icy in his veins. "It's Monoth!"

CHAPTER THREE

THE MONSTER FROM THE DEEP

Monoth surged up through the coral, swinging its massive head from side to side, its long pointed tusk ripping the branches to shreds like a hyperblade through strands of seaweed.

Max stared up in awe as the huge beast loomed above them, bigger than a ship, its flesh dark blue under Siborg's deadly armour.

The Robobeast's maddened red eyes glared down at them. Its mouth stretched wide, rimmed with deadly teeth.

Max gripped his hyperblade – but the weapon seemed puny and powerless in his hand.

I need to find a way to fight it!

As the great creature filled the sea above them, Max searched its powerful body for some sign of weakness. The head was armoured and the vast body was lined with rows of ferocious spikes. And the spinning tusk was a formidable weapon. Attacking Monoth would be like trying to storm a fortress!

I need more information… Max touched his wrist control.

"Roger? Can you see the Robobeast on your scanner?"

"I can," came Roger's shocked voice. "It's as big as a galleon!"

"Scan it for any sign of the Shell Helmet,"

Max told him urgently.

A few moments later, Roger's voice sounded again in Max's headset. "I can't be sure, but there's a hatch beneath the creature's left fin."

"The Shell Helmet must be there," said Max.

"I see another ship approaching!" Roger cried. "It's the *Hive*!"

Seconds later, the huge shape of the lab-ship pressed through the water above Max. Monoth flicked his monstrous tail, turning around and heading for Siborg's vessel.

We have to prevent Siborg from getting his hands on the Helmet. The price of failure would be the destruction of everything they cared about.

"Lia! Rivet!" Max shouted. "I'm sure Monoth has the Shell Helmet. It mustn't get to the *Hive*." He swam towards the huge Robobeast, Lia and Spike close by. Rivet sped upwards with his jets on full blast.

"Rivet attack Robobeast!" cried the dogbot.

"I'll fire on it from above," cried Roger.

Max saw torpedoes burst from the long dark shape of the *Lizard's Revenge*'s hull. They streaked through the water, leaving trails of foaming bubbles as they sped towards the Robobeast.

The torpedoes exploded on the Robobeast's thick metal armour and Max struggled against the blast-wave, his ears ringing with the noise as he fought against the frothing water.

He saw the Robobeast's mouth opening, its jagged teeth like rows of daggers as it roared in anger. There was new fury in the creature's red eyes as it slapped its long tail down and turned towards the *Lizard's Revenge*.

"Roger!" Max shouted. "It's coming for you. Get away as fast as you can!"

Lia was at Max's side, watching the Robobeast as it rushed upwards, its tusk whirling.

"Why isn't Roger moving the ship?" gasped Lia.

"The engines have died!" came Roger's desperate voice through the headset.

"Siborg must be using his tech-disrupter," Max shouted in despair. He stared up in horror as Monoth bore down on the helpless ship.

The monstrous Robobeast's tusk stabbed into the hull of the *Lizard's Revenge* with a deafening screech of gashed and ruptured metal. Air bubbles billowed through the water as the ship was torn apart.

"I have to try and help!" Max cried. He forced his body upwards through the water, every muscle straining as he swam towards the stricken ship.

"Are Roger and Grace still in there?" called Lia, straddling Spike's back as she followed Max. "Did they escape?"

"I don't know," Max replied, staring in horror as the Robobeast's drill punched into the hull of Roger's ship again, pushing it sideways through the churning water.

"Rivet find out!" The brave dogbot zoomed towards the surface.

"Be careful, Riv!' shouted Max. "Look for Roger and Grace in the water – keep them safe if you find them!"

Max felt a chill of pure terror as he saw Monoth lift his head. The Robobeast reared up, heaving the *Lizard's Revenge* clear of the sea. Then, as Max watched in disbelief, Monoth's tail flicked and the monstrous beast dived with the ship still impaled on its tusk.

If Grace and Roger are still aboard, they'll drown!

The sea filled with angry roars as Monoth tossed his head from side to side, trying to free his tusk from the ship's hull.

"Lia, this is our chance!" called Max. He pointed to a metal hatch in the Robobeast's armour that was visible just under its fin.

"We have to get the Helmet!"

The water foamed around the huge creature as they swam for the hatch. Max avoided the Robobeast's long, vicious spikes, but the creature's fin scythed through the water, forcing Max to dive as it swept close to his head.

Max dug the point of his hyperblade under the lid of the hatch and strained to break it open. But the lid would not come loose.

"Lia! Help me!"

Lia swam to his side, forcing her webbed fingers under the edge of the lid. Max again put all his strength into the hyperblade and suddenly the lid sprang open.

Inside the small locker, Max saw an ivory box, stained and dented and faded by the years.

It looks ancient.

"The Helmet must be inside!" cried Lia.

They dragged it from the locker and swam at full speed away from the enraged Robobeast.

Max glanced over his shoulder. Monoth had managed to get free of the *Lizard's Revenge*. The destroyed ship sank slowly to the seabed.

Max feared the worst. If Roger and Grace were inside, they were almost certainly…

"Look!" cried Lia. "They're alive!"

Max saw two figures – one larger than the other and both wearing deepsuits. It was Grace and Roger, swimming away from the wreckage of the *Lizard's Revenge*.

The Robobeast was climbing up to the surface.

Monoth must need to breathe air, like all whales, Max thought. *That gives us a small chance!*

"Max! More cyrates!" came Rivet's voice as the dogbot zipped towards them.

A stream of cyrates were emerging from chutes in the hull of the *Hive*.

Max's heart sank at this new peril. "We have to get out of here!" he shouted, kicking down towards the coral forest, the ivory box gripped in his hand.

Blaster bursts exploded around him as he swam towards his hydrodisk.

I have to take the Helmet as far away from here as possible.

He glimpsed Lia clinging to Spike's back as he darted rapidly among the cyrates. She was firing a blaster. Max guessed she must have taken it from one of the disabled cyrates. The cyrates were firing back, but the swordfish was too fast for them.

For the moment.

Max reached the hydrodisk. He was about to stow the box on board when a blast knocked it out of his hand, sending it tumbling across the seabed.

He saw it bounce safely into a tangle of seaweed. Several of the cyrates were heading straight for him.

I have to deal with them first!

Max jumped into the hydrodisk and engaged the engine. He steered towards the cyrates, slamming into them and sending

them spinning in all directions.

Above him, he could see Rivet darting through the water, blasting the cyrates with his rear thrusters as they chased after him. Roger and Grace had managed to grab one of the cyrates, and they were wrestling it as blaster bolts fired wildly. Roger stabbed a knife into the cyrate's neck and it went limp, its eyes flickering and then going dark.

Max smiled grimly. Slowly but surely, they were getting the better of Siborg's robots.

A massive explosion shook the water, almost ripping Max from the hydrodisk. He saw Lia fall from Spike's back as Rivet was sent tumbling. The seabed erupted in a gush of bubbles.

What was that?

An angry roaring came from above. Max stared up in time to see a second fiery blast burst from Monoth's tusk.

It isn't just a drill – it's a massive blaster!

The Robobeast had a weapon that could destroy them all.

CHAPTER FOUR

NO WAY OUT!

"Into the coral!" shouted Roger.

Good idea, thought Max. *We can outwit the cyrates in among the coral, and while Monoth searches for us, I'll have time to come up with a plan to defeat him.*

He dived for the coral forest, aware of Rivet speeding close by, and of Lia and Spike following.

But where was Grace?

"I'm not scared of you!" Max heard her shrill voice cry. The little girl was aiming a blaster rifle at the looming Robobeast.

Roger jetted towards her, the rocket boots of his deepsuit sending him through the water like an arrow.

"This is no time to be brave!" shouted Roger, grabbing Grace by the hand. He held her tightly as he zoomed down into the coral, closely pursued by several cyrates.

Max followed Roger and Grace in among the arching branches of coral as Monoth's blaster roared behind him.

Shards of coral exploded all around Max as he dodged the incoming fire. He could just make out the others ahead of him. Lia crouched low on Spike's back, calling out to the others.

"Keep close to me! Spike will find a way through."

Rivet zipped out from among the branches of coral up ahead to follow Spike.

Max sent the hydrodisk streaking off to avoid another lump of coral. But the rim cracked against a jutting stump, jarring his body painfully.

He gripped the throttle, twisting it beyond the safety mark. His eyes were fixed on the route ahead as he chased after his friends.

An explosion burst among the coral to

one side. Half blinded by the glare of its energy, Max spun the controls, turning the hydrodisk in the other direction.

Monoth only needs one lucky blast and we're done for.

The cyrates came threading through the tunnels on all sides, swarming among the coral, their blaster beams lancing the water.

Lia's voice sounded in his headset. "I'll get the Shell Helmet."

She and Spike veered off to one side.

"Be careful!" Max cried.

A spear of red fire sliced downwards, exploding among the coral with a deafening boom.

Monoth's blaster! Even Spike can't outrun that!

A desperate idea formed in Max's mind.

I've got no chance head-to-head with the Robobeast, but if I can get behind him....

He wrenched at the hydrodisk's controls, sending the disk in a giddying turn up and over and back along its own wake.

He darted through the coral, watching the huge shape of Monoth gliding above him. Thanks to Max's sudden change of direction, it looked like the creature had momentarily lost track of him. He twisted the grip on the handle and the hydrodisk shot up towards the Robobeast. At the last moment, he spun around, levelling the disk out and keeping it tight against the Robobeast's side.

I must find Monoth's control panel. If I can disable it, Siborg's power over the Robobeast will be gone.

Most of the Robobeast's force seemed to be focused in its tusk – hopefully the controls were there as well.

I need to distract him...

Max pressed the blaster button and locked

it on continuous fire mode. He jumped off the hydrodisk as the first volley of fire punched through the water and struck off the spikes that lined Monoth's flank.

"Well, well, Max." Siborg's sneering voice rang through his headset. "What do you think you're doing now?"

Max set his jaw.

The hydrodisk wasn't able to get past the armoured spikes, but its blasters were annoying the Robobeast. It twisted in the water, roaring with anger.

Lia was among the seaweed, far below, hunting frantically for the ivory box.

Max was about to swim towards the tusk to locate the control panel, when the

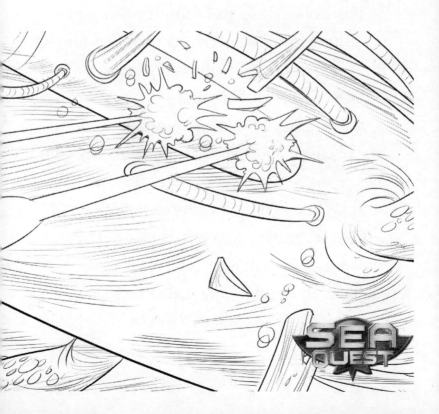

hydrodisk's blasters went silent.

"Had you forgotten my tech-disrupter?" crowed Siborg's voice in Max's ears. "Let's finish this little game. Monoth! Kill him!"

Turning towards Max, its red eyes burning with fury, Monoth gave a powerful flick of his tail and sent the disabled hydrodisk crashing to the seabed.

The Robobeast's vast mouth gaped open as it bore down on Max, its tusk churning the water as it spun with deadly speed.

Max twisted around, his muscles screaming for relief as he swam away from the onrushing Robobeast with all the speed he could muster. The water foamed all around him as the tusk approached.

Close to panic, Max dived more steeply, powering in among the coral, hoping desperately to find some shelter there.

I have to get clear – I need time to think!

He saw Roger, Grace and Rivet in the coral forest, fighting for their lives against the pitiless cyrates. The constant blaster fire of their attackers had them pinned behind a huge coral growth.

There was nothing Max could do to help them.

He glanced up, seeing the dark hull of the *Hive* hanging in the water above him.

Maybe Monoth will stop firing at me if I make for the Hive *– Siborg won't want those blasts coming too close to his ship!*

Hope and terror spurred him on to one last supreme effort. He sped through the coral branches, then kicked upwards, breaking into clear water. Battling the fatigue in his arms and legs, he swam for Siborg's ship.

"I see we have a visitor," came Siborg's sneering voice in Max's ears. "I must give you a proper welcome, Max."

Max watched in horror as hatches opened up in the lab-ship's hull. Blasters thrust out through the holes, every barrel turning to aim straight at him.

He slowed, treading water, his heart hammering.

He heard a hideous grinding noise behind him. He glanced back, seeing the monstrous form of Monoth hurtling towards him, the deadly tusk whirling, fangs gnashing, and murderous eyes ablaze.

Despair filled him, almost stopping his heart.

"Game over!" Siborg's voice was filled with vicious triumph. "All weapons… Fire!"

CHAPTER FIVE

VICTORY AND DEFEAT

The sea lit up with blaster fire, then Max felt something grab him, almost pulling his arm from its socket.

Lia!

Max felt the heat as Spike rode the shock wave of the *Hive*'s cannon fire. Streaks of energy boiled the water as the blasts struck the Robobeast, and Monoth disappeared behind a plume of scalding foam.

"Thank you," Max gasped as Spike slowed.

He stared back at the seething ball of bubbles. "Has the Robobeast been destroyed?"

"I hope not," said Lia. "It was an innocent creature, forced to do Siborg's will."

A ferocious roar came from the Robobeast and a flash of red flame hurtled towards the *Hive*. Monoth had survived, and now the creature was firing back.

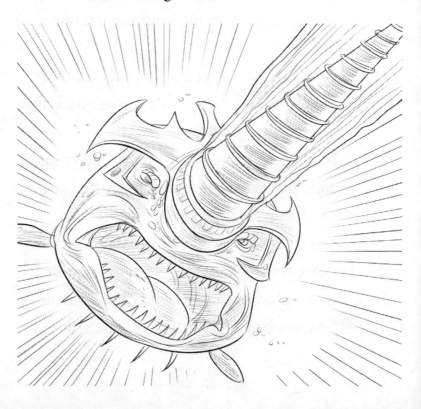

It thinks the Hive *is attacking it. That gives me the chance to try something.*

"Take me back to the Robobeast," Max said urgently, climbing onto Spike's back behind Lia. "We only have a few moments."

Lia urged Spike towards Monoth.

"To the tusk!" Max cried.

They sped along Monoth's back, avoiding the long spikes as they made for the armoured head.

Another high-powered blast erupted from the tusk, and the force of its impact rocked the *Hive.*

Max leaned from Spike's back, searching the tech-plating at the base of the tusk.

The control panel has to be here....

Max spotted something just behind the spinning tusk. "There!" he cried, pointing to a small metal box. Coiled wires trailed from the box, burrowing into the creature's flesh.

"I see it," said Lia.

Max flung himself from Spike's back, drawing his hyperblade and stabbing at the back of the box. It took him several tries before he could wedge the point of his blade behind the box. The muscles in his arms and shoulders burned with pain as he strained to rip the control box away from the creature's body.

"Got it!" he gasped as the box came loose and tumbled down the side of the Robobeast's head armour, long wires trailing.

The blaster stopped firing. Monoth gave a great shudder, wrenching his head from side to side. Max swam clear as the head armour broke apart and the rows of spikes dropped from the creature's flanks.

Monoth arched his back, his powerful tail lashing the water as the armoured plates fell to the ocean bed. He shook his head one final time and the loops of metal surrounding his tusk were shattered into pieces, the high-tech blaster breaking apart and falling away.

"He's not a Robobeast any more!" cried Lia. "You've broken Siborg's power over him."

Max swam downwards, looking into the creature's eyes. They were no longer red, no longer filled with rage.

But before Max could move, the gigantic narwhal's eyes fixed on him and it opened its massive jaws.

For a terrifying moment, as he stared at the rows of pointed teeth, Max thought the creature was going to attack him. But a beautiful, eerie song burst out of the creature's mouth, echoing through the water.

"He's thanking us for saving him," cried Lia, her eyes shining. "Well done, Max!"

"We're not done yet." Monoth had been deprogrammed, but the lab-ship was still intact and some of Siborg's cyrates were still undefeated.

He stared down into the coral forest, touching the communications button on his headset. "Rivet? Roger? Grace? Are you there? Come in, please!"

But all he heard was static.

What happened down there while I was fighting Monoth?

He saw some movement among the branching coral below.

It's a cyrate – and it looks badly damaged.

The robot pirate rose from the coral, one arm torn away at the elbow, exposed wires hanging from its chest. Its head was blackened by blaster fire and one eye was dark.

It was carrying something in its one remaining hand.

"The ivory chest!" cried Lia.

"I'll stop it!" Max swam towards the cyrate

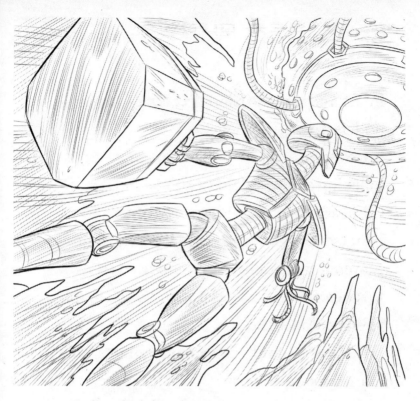

as it headed for the *Hive*.

Fear and determination spurred him on. He hurtled through the water, swimming faster than he had ever swum in his life, straining every sinew in his body. If Siborg got the final piece of the Arms of Addulis, all would be lost!

But the cyrate put on a last spurt of speed and vanished into one of the chutes that sprouted from the lab-ship's hull.

"I'm going in after it!" Max said grimly into his headset.

"Be careful!" said Lia.

But Max knew this was no time for caution. He had to risk everything. Once Siborg powered up his ship, he would head straight for the undersea city of Sumara to begin his reign of destruction.

"I'll ask Monoth to keep Siborg busy," said Lia. "Good luck."

Max glanced back and saw Lia close to the narwhal's head, her lips moving silently as she used her Aqua Powers to speak to the huge creature. A moment later, Monoth swam towards the lab-ship's side.

Good! That will give me the time I need.

Max aimed for the chute that the damaged cyrate had used. As he entered the lab-ship, he heard a loud bang and the walls around him shuddered. *Monoth must be butting up against the hull.*

Max noticed that Siborg's taunts had stopped coming from his headset.

For the first time on this Quest, things aren't going entirely his way.

A metal sheet blocked the chute. Max ran his hand across a wall-pad and the sheet slid aside, allowing him to swim into an airlock. The sheet closed behind him and the water drained quickly away. He activated a second pad and another hatch opened ahead of him.

He stepped through the doorway and drew his hyperblade, ready to fight for his life.

But there was no sign of the damaged cyrate who'd been carrying the ivory box.

He'll have taken the Helmet straight to Siborg. I have to act fast.

Max ducked through a bulkhead doorway and ran along a narrow, curving corridor.

He hoped that he could remember the *Hive*'s layout from the last time he had been aboard. If he was right, this route would lead him to the cavernous room where the cyrates were stored.

He reached the door and gripped his hyperblade tighter before stepping inside. To his relief, he found the chamber empty. Siborg must have called all his minions to battle stations.

That was a mistake, Siborg, Max thought grimly. *And I'm going to make you pay dearly for it.*

He rushed to a control panel set into the wall. Working rapidly, he activated the guidance and power systems.

"I know a hack that will shut the whole ship down," he muttered under his breath.

His fingers moved at lightning speed, closing down one power grid after another.

A final tap and the lights in the massive room went out.

The lab-ship was dead in the water!

But as he turned from the control panel, a dozen red laser sights struck at him out of the gloom. He squinted, trying to see the source of the beams. He lifted his hyperblade.

Max heard a metallic footstep and a split second later pain flared in his head and he knew nothing more.

CHAPTER SIX

THE TRUTH AT LAST

"Max, are you there? Please answer me!"

Max became aware of Lia's anxious voice in his ears. He winced, pain lancing through his head. He was face down – but not on the ground. His arms and legs were being held in pincer-like grips.

He opened his eyes and saw the floor moving beneath him. He struggled fiercely, but the hands of four cyrates tightened on his wrists and ankles.

What had happened? He tried to gather his thoughts.

He remembered the red laser lights. He must have been surrounded by cyrates just after cutting the power.

I was knocked out.

The lights were back on now. Siborg must have reactivated the power core.

All Max's hopes had been dashed – and now he was a helpless prisoner in the *Hive*. He gritted his teeth, summoning up every last reserve of courage and strength.

No! Not helpless – not while there was breath in his body!

The cyrates carried him through a doorway and flung him to the floor.

Max turned onto his back, stifling a cry of pain. He was in a brightly lit room filled with high-tech consoles and workstations, manned by cyrates. He saw with a sinking heart that one of them held his hyperblade.

A transparent bubble-screen showed a wide stretch of open ocean.

I'm on the bridge, he thought, clambering to his feet. He staggered to catch his balance, still dazed from the blow to his head.

Through the bubble-screen he could see chunks of Monoth's armour floating in the water.

"At least I defeated the Robobeast," he muttered.

"Yes, you won that battle."

Max spun around at the sound of Siborg's voice. His enemy was standing at a computer bank, his face hidden from Max within the helmet of the huge, lumbering battle suit he wore – a robotic exoskeleton. "But you lost the war."

One huge hand of the battle suit clutched

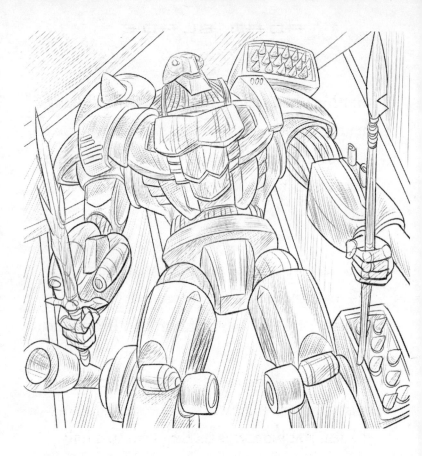

the Sword of Addulis; the other held the Pearl Spear. The Stone Breastplate hung from the suit's broad, powerful shoulders.

"Monoth served his purpose," Siborg continued. "He found the fourth of the ancient Arms of Addulis." He gestured with his sword-arm towards the damaged cyrate that Max had followed into the *Hive*. "Bring me the chest!"

The cyrate limped forwards, its one remaining hand still clinging to the ivory chest.

"At last!" Greed filled Siborg's voice as he laid the weapons aside. "Open it and give me the Shell Helmet!"

Max eyed the sword and spear. If only he could reach them!

He took a single step, but a blast of fire from one of the battle suit's weapons burned the floor at his feet, bringing him to a halt.

"Stay right where you are," said Siborg. "I don't want to kill you just yet."

Max stared at Siborg in silent anger.

All I can do is wait and hope that Lia finds some way to help me.

The cyrate opened the lid of the chest and took out the Shell Helmet. It was white, shaped like a conch shell and rimmed with curling ridges. A long gnarled spike stood up from its top.

Siborg took the Helmet in both hands. He turned away, and Max saw the top of the battle suit open up. The arms lifted and the Helmet was lowered inside.

Who or what are you, Siborg? Why are you so afraid to show yourself?

"Soon I shall feel the power coursing through me," said Siborg as the battle suit closed again and he turned towards Max. "I will be able to control every creature in the ocean! I will be invincible."

No! This is not over yet! Maybe I can still force his hand.

"You're a coward," cried Max. "You hide away inside that suit, ordering your cyrates to do your dirty work for you!"

"That's what technology is for," came the

careless reply. "Or are you like those witless, backward Merryn – afraid of technology's power?"

"I'm not afraid of it," Max said, clenching his fists in fury. "I believe in its power to do good – unlike you!"

"That's because you're a fool." A bitter laugh came from the battle suit. "I know better!"

Max glanced towards the bubble-screen, hoping his friends were still alive. They would not desert him. They would be making plans to save the day. He just hoped they wouldn't do anything reckless.

But the sea was filled with swarms of silvery cyrates, cruising around the lab-ship like deadly fish.

"You're looking for your allies," scoffed Siborg. "They've all run away. You're a fool to trust beings of flesh and blood – only programming and robotics can be relied upon."

"You're wrong," snarled Max. "And your lack of faith in people will be your downfall."

"I think not," said Siborg. "Cyrates! Power up the engines. Set a course for Sumara. We will destroy the Merryn city first and then we'll make our way to Aquora. I want our guest to watch as I lay waste to that underwater slag-tip and then smash his glorious home city to rubble!"

Max lunged forward, but two cyrates grabbed his arms, pulling him back and pinning him to a wall. "What have those people ever done to you?" he cried in outrage.

"They have done everything!" growled Siborg.

"They'll fight you," Max shouted. "Aquora will defend itself to the last person!"

"I hope they do," said Siborg. "I will enjoy

watching every one of them die." He turned to Max. "Haven't you realised yet? Nothing can stop me. My tech-disrupter will disable the city's defensive shields and then I will pound it to ruins with my blasters."

Rage gave Max a last surge of strength. He ripped free of the cyrates, and lunged for the robot that was holding his hyperblade. He tore the weapon from its fingers and with a cry of anger, he flung himself at Siborg.

All the cyrates on the bridge turned to him, blasters in their hands.

"No!" commanded Siborg, snatching up the Sword and the Spear of Addulis. "Leave him to me!" Immediately, every cyrate lowered its weapon, but their cold red eyes were still fixed on Max.

He gripped his hyperblade in both hands, balancing himself as the hulking battle suit advanced on him.

It's just you and me now, Siborg!

Siborg stabbed with the Spear and brought the sword around in a great scything arc. Max leaped above the blade, sweeping his own sword down to block the blow, then twisted in midair and struck the Spear aside.

He ducked another slash of the Sword, but the Spear jabbed down and he had to fling himself into a forward roll to avoid being impaled on the lethal tip. He sprang to his feet, his hyperblade gripped in both hands as he searched his enemy for weak spots.

I have to get closer! Tech can be disabled! Siborg is a fool to put all his trust in it!

Maybe the joint between the shoulders and the helmet was a vulnerable point. If he could strike a clean blow there, Siborg would be driven back.

I might even sever some vital wiring!

He launched himself forwards, dodging

the swinging Sword and the darting Spear. He hacked at the Breastplate with all his strength, but his hyperblade glanced off, jarring his arms and throwing him off balance. Siborg smashed into Max's side with the fist holding the Coral Sword, hurling him to the ground. A great armoured foot

stomped down on Max's hyperblade, jerking it out of his fingers.

Siborg lunged with the Pearl Spear as Max squirmed from side to side to avoid the lethal tip.

The point of the Coral Sword pressed down on his chest.

"Make one more move and I'll pin you to the deck!" Siborg snarled.

Max lay still, lights swimming round his head as he fought for breath. "This is pathetic!" snarled Siborg, thrusting the Spear into the battle suit's belt and bending down to catch Max's ankle in a vice-like metal fist.

Siborg wrenched Max into the air, holding him upside down. Max writhed wildly, trying to free himself.

"Any last requests?" said Siborg, drawing back the Coral Sword.

"I want to know who you are!" cried Max.

"And I want to know why you are so full of hatred!"

The sword arm paused.

"My father made me who I am," Siborg said.

"Who is your father?" demanded Max.

"Oh, you know him well," snarled Siborg, his fingers gnawing into Max's ankle.

"Tell me his name!" cried Max.

Siborg spoke slowly. "You call him…the Professor!"

CHAPTER SEVEN

THE POWER OF THE SHELL HELMET

"Your father is my uncle?" gasped Max. *He must be lying! My uncle didn't have any children.*

"Yes, he is," said Siborg. "And that makes you my cousin."

Max twisted in Siborg's grip. The blood thundered in his head as he hung upside down, completely defenceless.

"Father never wanted me because my

mother was Merryn." Siborg's voice was sour. Max was lifted higher, the fist squeezing his ankle painfully. "Even as a child, I was too much of a Breather for the Merryn, and too Merryn to fit into the world of humans."

Max stared at where he thought Siborg's head must be inside the battle suit. He felt a pang of pity for him. *It must have been horrible to grow up knowing he didn't fit in anywhere.*

"I'm sorry," Max said. "But killing all those people won't make you feel better." He caught his breath. "I can talk to them for you. I'll make them understand."

The hand shook him roughly. Pain shot through his body, making the blood ring in his ears.

"It's too late for that," Siborg said. "They have made me the person I am. Soon, they will see the results – when I destroy them."

But Max noticed the sword had dropped a little.

"I understand how you must feel," he said. He had to try and talk his murderous cousin down. Backed up by his tech-weapons and his army of cyrates, Siborg was capable of killing thousands of innocent people.

"How could you possibly understand?" said Siborg.

"You're right," gasped Max, fighting against a growing dizziness as he hung upside down. "I can't know what it's like to have grown up alone – but I can try and understand, if you'll talk to me about it."

The grip on Max's ankle loosened a little but when Siborg spoke, his voice was scornful. "Why should you care about me?" he asked. "We are enemies, cousin. You're playing for time because you fear me!"

"Of course I fear you," said Max. "But we needn't be enemies. The same blood runs through our veins. The blood that comes from your father and my mother – your aunt. I know she would love you just as she loves me."

"Love?" shrieked Siborg, the hydraulic fingers closing with bone-grinding force around Max's ankle. "Love is weakness. I will show you the power of hate!"

Siborg's fingers tightened on the Sword of Addulis and he lifted his arm high. "Your loving parents shall have you back!" he yelled. "One piece for each of them!"

All hope was gone. Max steeled himself for death. He had failed the people of Nemos – and this time there was no escape.

But before Siborg could bring the sword down, the *Hive* tilted wildly to one side and he staggered as he tried to keep his footing. The cyrates stumbled across the floor, some of them falling as the lab-ship teetered for a moment then rocked back again.

Max dropped out of Siborg's grasp. He managed to cushion the fall with his arms. His foot was numb from the battle suit's grip, but he pulled himself across the bridge, desperate to get out of Siborg's reach.

Alarms blared as the lab-ship rocked again. Control panels and consoles hissed, spitting sparks and gushing plumes of smoke.

"What's happening?" shouted Siborg.

He stomped over to a scanner, brushing a cyrate aside with one arm. "There are creatures in the coral forest," Siborg snarled.

Max got to his feet and stared through the viewing panel in amazement. The trunks and limbs of coral were moving, uncurling, stretching out. Deep-set eyes opened in craggy faces. Backs unbent as great shapes rose from the seabed. The coral was coming alive.

"The giants are waking up!" shouted Max, remembering the strange tale Lia had told him about the coral forest. "They won't let you destroy Nemos!"

"They are creatures of the sea!" shouted Siborg. "And I am wearing the Shell Helmet. I will force them to obey me!" His voice rose to

a shout. "I order you to stop!"

Max could see from the scanner that the whole of the seabed was alive now with gigantic humanoid shapes. They swam up and clamped themselves to the hull of the *Hive*.

"Why aren't they obeying me?" howled

Siborg. "Cyrates! Defend my ship!"

The lab-ship tipped forwards as the coral giants clambered over the hull, tearing off armour plates and ripping blasters from their hatches.

Max watched the giants in awe. Their massive, hulking bodies were gnarled and knobbed with ancient growth, their long limbs jutting out at odd angles, their many-fingered hands reaching out like iron clamps. They had great, blunt heads with heavy brows and dark eyes. Their wide mouths stretched open as they roared, revealing rows of huge square teeth.

Even as Max stared at the screen, he saw ranks of cyrates shooting through the sea, attacking the giants with their blasters. The giants turned on the cyrates, flailing their massive limbs, swatting the robots like flies. The sea was criss-crossed with blaster rays, as the giants snatched at the cyrates, crushing them, ripping them to pieces.

But the cyrates fought back; blaster-fire exploded across the giants' bodies, sending hunks of coral flying through the water.

Max watched the battle helplessly.

I should be out there! But if he tried to escape he would be cut down by the cyrates that surrounded him.

"I am wearing the Shell Helmet!" raged Siborg, staring at the screen. "Why do the creatures of the sea not obey me?" He raised his fists. "Come to my aid, all sea creatures! In the name of Addulis, I command it!"

Max's blood ran cold as he saw shapes moving through the water towards them. It was a whole host of creatures – octopuses, sharks, dolphins, stingrays... hundreds of them racing in from all directions.

The Shell Helmet was working! And soon

the coral giants would be overwhelmed.

But then something strange began to happen. The sea creatures set about attacking the cyrates! Octopus tentacles latched onto metal limbs, sharks buried their teeth in robotic carcasses, and stingrays sent electric shocks through the stricken robots.

Max gave a whoop of astonished delight.

"No!" shrieked Siborg, beating at the screen with his fists. "This cannot be happening! You must obey me!"

A path opened through the pitched battle and Max saw Lia, riding on Spike's back, flanked by Rivet and surrounded by a bodyguard of sharks. Upon her head she was wearing a helmet of her own.

Max stared in amazement. The helmet was beautiful! It glowed with a lustrous mother-of-pearl sheen. It was crested with tall, horned spikes, and its inside gleamed with gold. It made the helmet Siborg was wearing look like a tawdry copy.

That has to be the real Shell Helmet! But how?

Max heard a sudden explosion behind him. He spun around. A plume of smoke billowed into the bridge. Roger and Grace ran through the smoke, both of them holding blasters.

"Surrender, you scurvy knave!" shouted Grace, pointing her blaster at Siborg. "Your

helmet is just a fake!"

"No!" howled Siborg.

"Grace switched them," cried Roger. "The one you're wearing is a piece of junk we found in the hold of the *Lizard's Revenge*. Grace made the swap while the box was lying in the seaweed." He aimed his blaster at the battle suit's chest. "You've been outwitted by a little girl, Siborg. It's time to give in!"

CHAPTER EIGHT

COUNTDOWN TO DEATH

"I will never surrender!" With a bellow of rage, Siborg swung the Pearl Spear at the bubble-screen, shattering the glass to flying fragments.

Seawater gushed into the bridge, crashing through the cyrates, pouring over the control consoles and swirling across the floor. Sparks and plumes of smoke jetted up as the instruments were submerged.

Max was knocked to the floor by the

torrent. He saw Roger catch hold of Grace as the flood struck them, sweeping them off their feet. Cyrates were thrown around, helpless against the pressure of the swirling water.

The surge smashed against the far wall, the whole of the bridge filling with churning seawater. Helpless fish were sucked in by the turmoil and pieces of coral spun, ricocheting off the walls.

Fighting against the pressure, Max saw that Siborg was still on his feet. Bubbles erupted under the battle suit's boots and he rose from the floor on powerful thrusters.

He dived headfirst through the shattered screen. Max fought through the water to follow him. A cyrate blocked his way, but he swung his hyperblade and cut the robot aside, its broken chest trailing wires.

He swam out into the open ocean. All

around him, the ferocious battle raged. He saw Rivet fighting alongside the coral giants and the sea creatures. Siborg rocketed through the towering giants, blasting at them, trying to force his way through, but there were too many. One huge hand snatched hold of his foot, while another giant rose up in front of him, its mouth stretching wide in anger as its fist crashed down on the battle suit's chest.

The vengeful giants closed in around Siborg until all that Max could see were occasional blasts shooting out from between their coral limbs.

It's like a feeding frenzy, Max thought as the giants began to rip at the battle suit. Broken pieces of armour and weaponry floated free. For all his high-tech, Siborg was no match for these ancient creatures.

The Coral Sword of Addulis cartwheeled through the water. Soon afterwards, the

Breastplate drifted away. And then, finally,
Max saw the Pearl Spear sinking slowly
towards the seabed.

"Help me!" Max heard a weak voice through his headset.

Max swam over to where Lia was watching the battle, sitting astride Spike and surrounded by sharks.

"Call the giants off," Max said. "They'll kill him."

"Help me, please!" said Siborg again.

Lia stared into Max's eyes and for a moment he was afraid she would refuse. After all, Siborg had brought terrible pain to the ocean and its creatures. But then she turned and closed her eyes. "Cease your attack," she said quietly.

The giants drew back, leaving the twisted and ruined battle suit floating amidst wires, cables and other pieces of debris.

Max swam down through the giants, seeing no sign of movement from Siborg. He feared the worst.

Then he saw a hand twitch feebly. He moved in closer. The viewing panel was cracked and dented. Max pushed his fingers behind the panel and prised it open.

He gasped in shock at the pale, wounded face that stared out at him. The face of a boy, not much older than Max.

Siborg's features were half hidden behind riveted metal plating, leaving only one eye visible. Brown hair tumbled over the metal implants, almost covering a glowing red laser eye.

That's why the pirates of the Chaos Quadrant called him Red Eye.

Max stared in horror. Wires stuck out from a long cut along his cousin's cheek. Cables and electronic devices ran down Siborg's neck, engaging with yet more high-tech devices clamped to his shoulders and chest.

What has Siborg done to himself? How much

of him is still human?

Gills opened and closed weakly under the boy's ears. Max didn't know whether to feel pity or disgust at the way Siborg had turned himself into this hideous robot hybrid.

Siborg's remaining human eye glowered at Max with undisguised hatred.

"Kill me," Siborg murmured from between gritted teeth. "Do it while you have the chance. If you spare me, you know I'll seek revenge."

"Perhaps you will," said Max gently. "But I can't kill you. You're hurt and you have no weapons." He looked closely into his cousin's eye. "There's good in you deep down, I know it. We don't have to be enemies."

"You're wrong," spat Siborg. "There is no good in me at all – I lost it long ago."

"You tricked me into handing over the Arms of Addulis by pretending there was a bomb attached to Grace's ankle," Max reminded him. "But remember what you said to me? You said you would never hurt a child. That proves you have a conscience." Max gazed into the ruined face. "Just because your father is wicked and cruel, that doesn't mean you have to be. I'll take you back to Aquora. You can have a real home there."

Siborg smiled, his robo-arm lifting.

For a moment, Max thought Siborg was going to make some gesture of friendship, but then the hand moved to the chest panel, opened a small domed cover and flipped a switch.

"What have you done?" Max asked.

"I've activated the suit's self-destruct function," Siborg said calmly. "You have thirty seconds to escape."

"No!" Max reached for the switch, but Siborg closed the lid and pressed down onto it. Max frantically tried to pull the hand free.

"Goodbye, cousin," Siborg said quietly.

Still Max fought against the robotic hand. If he could get to the switch, he could stop the self-destruct countdown. He stabbed his hyperblade down behind the metal fingers, using all his strength and weight to try and tear it loose.

Hands snatched at Max from behind.

"You have to get away from him!" cried Lia.

"I can save him!" shouted Max.

"It's too late for that." Roger had hold of him as well. Max struggled frantically as he was pulled away from his cousin.

"You're a fool, Max!" Siborg laughed softly. "Will you never learn?" The robo-hand touched another switch. "Say hello to my father!" The top of the battle suit split open with a loud crack.

"He's escaping!" shouted Roger as Siborg ejected from the suit and shot upwards on explosive rocket boots.

Max stared upwards in dismay. He heard

Siborg's mocking laughter echoing through his communicator headset as his cousin sped away through the water.

CHAPTER NINE

BLOOD ENEMIES

Max watched Siborg disappear, leaving a thin wake of bubbles as he vanished into the open ocean.

"Should we pursue him?" cried Roger.

"No," Max said wearily. "Let him go."

I think we'll meet again. I just hope it won't be as enemies.

Lia raised her arms. "Go now, my friends," she called to the sea creatures that still swam around them. "Thank you for your help."

All the animals glided quietly away into

the sea. A strange hush came over the ocean. The battle was over. Not one cyrate remained active. Pieces of the robots drifted eerily in the water: arms, legs and severed heads trailing dead wiring.

The coral giants stood on the seabed in a great, solemn circle, watching Lia like soldiers

waiting for commands from their leader.

She raised her arms in a salute to them. "You have done well, Warriors of Addulis," she called. "Sleep now, until you are needed again."

Wordlessly, the giants lay down, their arms stretching up, their fingers widening like branches, their legs becoming no more than arches of living coral. Their bodies interlocked and fused together as they stiffened. The forest became still. The giants were asleep once more.

Lia removed the Shell Helmet, her silver hair floating free. Max and the rest of the battle-weary companions gathered around her.

"We beat Siborg," said Grace. "But it's a shame the *Lizard's Revenge* got scuttled."

Roger put his hand to his chest. "A piece of my heart went down with her, shipmates," he sighed. "She was a gallant vessel. I'll never forget her."

"Admit it, Roger – are you more upset about the ship or the treasure?" asked Lia with a grin.

"A bit of both, Princess," said Roger.

"The Arms of Addulis are down among the coral. We need to get them and put them all somewhere really safe," Max said to the others. "And I think I know the perfect place."

Max drained his cup, smiling as he gazed around the crowded throne room of Sumara. Tables filled the long chamber, laden with the richest food and drink in the city. Hundreds of the Merryn folk had been called to the Royal Palace, and all the faces Max could see were merry and joyful.

King Salinus rose from his throne. "This celebration has been called to give thanks to

our guests of honour," he cried. "All praise to Max and to my daughter Lia." He raised his cup. "To Roger, and to little Grace too!"

There was a mighty cheer from the revellers.

"Don't forget Rivet!" Grace called.

"And Rivet," agreed the King, turning to the Arms of Addulis that hung on the wall behind him. "These brave companions found the Sword, Spear, Breastplate and Shell Helmet." He raised a hand to quieten the applause. "The Arms will be locked deep below the city, guarded night and day so that they will never again fall into the hands of our enemies."

To tumultuous applause the King sat, taking the hand of Lia, who was sitting with Max and the others at the top table.

"Father, what can you tell us about Siborg?" she asked. "He told Max he has a Merryn mother."

The King's cheeks burned red. "It is true," he said. "I knew of the child, but I never thought the old story had any connection to the man called Red Eye." He sighed. "My people behaved shamefully. But in those days there was little trust of Breathers."

"But what happened?" asked Max.

"Long ago, your uncle met a Sumaran

woman and fell in love with her – or at least, he claimed he was in love," said the King. "A child was born to them. The woman wished to rear the child with its father in Aquora, but the Professor spurned her." He shook his head sadly. "She returned to Sumara with the boy, whom she named Simon. He was able to breathe in water and in air and she hoped they would find a welcome here. Alas, it was not to be. They settled in Astar, on the outskirts of the city. But they were treated as outcasts, the boy bullied, the woman ignored."

Max listened with growing sadness as he tried to imagine Simon's miserable life.

"The boy stopped attending school," the King continued. "He spent all his time in the Graveyard where my people discard all the technological devices they dislike."

Max frowned. "I imagine Simon was

already experimenting on himself by then," he said with a shudder. "Making terrible changes to himself."

"Indeed," said the King.

"He looked more than half robotic," murmured Max. "He must have hated himself to do that!"

The King nodded grimly. "Then one day he simply disappeared, and we knew nothing more of him."

"That must be when he joined the pirates in the Chaos Quadrant," said Max.

"His poor mother died of grief," murmured the King under his breath. "It was a sad and lonely death."

"I blame my uncle for this," Max said angrily. "How could he have abandoned his own child like that?"

Siborg's was a tragic tale, but no matter how cruel his cousin's upbringing, it didn't excuse his behaviour.

Still, there must be good in him. If we meet again, I'll do everything I can to find it!

After the feast, Max left Lia with her father in the Palace and headed to the outskirts of Sumara, where Roger and Grace were waiting with Max's hydrodisk.

"What plans do you have?" Max asked Roger. He gave a quick half-smile. "Steal another ship, perhaps?"

Roger's eyebrows shot up. "As if I'd ever dream of such a thing," he said.

"Let's go back to the Chaos Quadrant, Uncle," piped Grace, tugging his sleeve. "Now old Red Eye is gone, we can have a lot of fun there."

Roger looked at her. "I seem to remember Max promised us a guided tour of Aquora."

"Yes," cried Grace. "And those nasty cyrate

things attacked the city before we even got started." She looked up at Max with a big grin. "How about it, shipmate? Do we get our tour?"

Max laughed as he looked around at his friends. "It will be my pleasure," he said. "And let's hope this time we're not interrupted!"

Don't miss Max's next Sea Quest adventure,

when he faces

FLIKTOR
THE DEADLY FROG

SEA QUEST ®

Look out for all the books in
Sea Quest Series 6:

MASTER OF AQUORA

FLIKTOR THE DEADLY FROG
TENGAL THE SAVAGE SHARK
KULL THE CAVE CRAWLER
GULAK THE GULPER EEL

Don't miss the
BRAND NEW
Special Bumper
Edition:

OCTOR
MONSTER OF THE DEEP

COMING SOON!

WIN AN EXCLUSIVE GOODY BAG

In every Sea Quest book the Sea Quest logo is hidden in one of the pictures. Find the logos in books 17-20, make a note of which pages they appear on and go online to enter the competition at

www.seaquestbooks.co.uk

Each month we will put all of the correct entries into a draw and select one winner to receive a special Sea Quest goody bag.

You can also send your entry on a postcard to:

Sea Quest Competition, Orchard Books,
338 Euston Road, London, NW1 3BH

Don't forget to include your name and address!

GOOD LUCK

Closing Date: 30th April 2015

IF YOU LIKE SEA QUEST, YOU'LL LOVE BEAST QUEST!

Series 1: COLLECT THEM ALL!

An evil wizard has enchanted the magical beasts of Avantia. Only a true hero can free the beasts and save the land. Is Tom the hero Avantia has been waiting for?

978 1 84616 483 5

978 1 84616 482 8

978 1 84616 484 2

978 1 84616 486 6

978 1 84616 485 9

978 1 84616 487 3